D0468519

NO LONGER PROPERTY OF
SEATTLE PUBLIC LIBRARY

That's Not Normal!
is selected by the prestigious
White Ravens catalog.

To Valentina,
Soon reading will become the
most normal thing in the world for you.
Mar Pavón

To my son, Youenn.
Laure du Faÿ

ÉGALITƎ

That's Not Normal!
Egalité Series

© Text: Mar Pavón, 2014
© Illustrations: Laure du Faÿ, 2015
© Edition: NubeOcho, 2021
www.nubeocho.com · info@nubeocho.com

Original title: *¡Eso no es normal!*
English translation: Martin Hyams
Text editing: Teddi Rachlin, Caroline Dookie, Rebecca Packard

First published in 2015 by NubeOcho.
First edition in this format: November 2021
ISBN: 978-84-18133-23-7
Legal Deposit: M-31695-2020

Printed in Portugal.

All rights reserved.

THAT'S NOT NORMAL!

Mar Pavón

Laure du Faÿ

nubeOCHO

Elephant had a very, very long trunk... Incredibly long!

"That's not normal!"

He used it to **shower** and **blow dry** Baby Elephant.

"That's not normal!"

He helped **Old Monkey** to climb the trees.

"That's not normal!"

He rocked Little Antelope to sleep.

"That's not normal!"

He helped to hang Zebra's stripes to dry.

"That's not normal!"

He wrapped up Giraffe's neck to keep it warm.

"That's not normal!"

Almost all the animals were grateful to Elephant for his kindness. Only **Hippopotamus** made sure to remind everyone that elephant's long nose...

Wasn't normal!

One day while Hippopotamus was staring at Elephant's long trunk, he didn't realize that Baby Hippo had gotten out of the pond to follow a grasshopper.

Such a fast hippopotamus had never been seen before!
The alarmed animals **yelled out**:

"That's not normal!"

"That can't be good!"

"That's going to end badly!"

"We have to tell Hippopotamus to do something!"

Hippopotamus heard the shouting and wanted
to find out what was going on.

Elephant, also alerted by the cries, rushed over with
his **trunk coiled up** to avoid **stumbling**. Hippopotamus
didn't hesitate to trip him up as he passed by.

Elephant fell heavily on the sand and Hippopotamus started making fun of him:

"Look, look! **Clumsy Elephant** tripped over his **trunk** and fell flat on his face!"

But the animals arriving from the other side were not laughing. "Come on, Hippopotamus, hurry! Your **baby** is chasing a **grasshopper** and heading towards the **lake**!"

On hearing that, Hippopotamus panicked, and with good reason: the lake was full of **hungry crocodiles!**

Hippopotamus raced off, followed by his neighbors.
They all wanted to **rescue** Baby Hippo.

Baby Hippo, still chasing the grasshopper, was getting dangerously close to the lake. Several pairs of glassy eyes were lurking in the water, **waiting...**

Hippopotamus ran and ran... But his baby, exhausted and sweaty, jumped into the **lake** to cool off, unaware of the danger!

A pair of floating eyes approached Baby Hippo...
Another pair followed. And a third pair began to close in.

The little one's fate seemed set...

But suddenly, miraculously, Elephant's trunk got there first.
The trunk plunged silently into the water and...
WHAM! In a flash, Baby Hippo was hauled up.

This unexpected move baffled the **crocodiles.** They eagerly opened their massive mouths for **three** awesome **bites...**

of air!

Hippopotamus felt sorry he had been so mean to Elephant
and **thanked him** for saving his baby.

He **apologized** and promised not to judge anyone for being **different**.

And everything went back to normal...

Or did it?